W9-CRQ-769

Conejos Library District
Maria De Herrera Branch

R.I.F.

# Stray

by
LYNN
HALL

*illustrations by Joseph Cellini*

**AVON BOOKS**
A division of
The Hearst Corporation
959 Eighth Avenue
New York, New York 10019

**Text Copyright © 1974 by Lynn Hall.**
**Illustrations Copyright © 1974 by Follett Publishing Company.**
Published by arrangement with Follett Publishing Company.
Library of Congress Catalog Card Number: 73-90053.

ISBN 0-380-00202-7

All rights reserved, which includes the right to reproduce
this book or portions thereof in any form whatsoever.
For information address Follett Publishing Company,
1010 West Washington Boulevard, Chicago, Illinois 60607.

**First Camelot Printing, March, 1975.**

CAMELOT TRADEMARK REG. U.S. PAT. OFF. AND IN
OTHER COUNTRIES, MARCA REGISTRADA, HECHO EN U.S.A.

Printed in the U.S.A.

# Stray

LYNN HALL loves dogs, and she loves to write. For several years she has devoted herself full-time to writing books for young readers, most of them fictional stories about dogs.

Ms. Hall was born in a suburb of Chicago and was raised in Des Moines, Iowa. She has always loved dogs and horses and has kept them around her whenever possible. As a child, she was limited to stray dogs, neighbor's horses, and the animals found in library books. In recent years she has realized her lifelong dream of owning her own kennel and raising her own dogs. She now lives in the village of Masonville, Iowa.

# Chapter 1

THE DOG lay in the shade of a boulder, panting and watching the town below him. He had just come over the top of the bluff and started down its steep side, weaving among low cedar trees and limestone ledges. But the sight of the town below had stopped him. He would go down and explore it eventually, but for now he preferred high solitude.

He was a large, rangy dog with lines that suggested setter blood. His black coat was dust-dulled and bulging with burr-hearted mats and tags of dead winter hair. His lips, drawn back in a panting smile, revealed teeth that bore the brown marks of puppyhood distemper suffered and survived.

For the past few weeks his course had been roughly eastward, bearing to the south when detours were necessary. There had been long stays, sometimes two or three weeks, where the living was comfortable. Now, in the northeast corner of Iowa, he was beginning to feel a lessening of the eastward pull. The river was close now. The river meant fish tossed to him by silent rubber-booted men. Clams. Children with crusts of sandwiches to trade for a chance to pet him.

He sat up against the boulder, tensed, then dug furiously into his ear with his hind foot, bursting a blood-filled tick with his toenails and smearing the blood on ear and foot. Angrily he rubbed the ear against his foreleg; then, avenged, he settled back into the mulch of oak leaves and soft cedar needles. Sighing, groaning with comfort, he placed his chin in the trough between his forelegs and allowed his eyes to close.

For all practical purposes, Scotia was a ghost town. Its handful of buildings were strung along the foot of the bluff and held together by the old highway. The new highway, three miles to the south, had taken away the village's last small excuse for living.

There were only three live houses now, twice as many dead ones, an empty fake-brick post office, and Melkies' Groceries, Gas, and Beer. Then there was the surprisingly well-groomed Scotia Lutheran Church. The church owed much of its care to the rivalry between Pearl Schmidt and Ora French. The women were sisters, but there had been little love between them for the past twenty years, since Ora married first and was given the larger of the two farmhouses their parents owned. Pearl tried to show her superiority by having newer furniture than Ora, and by working harder on church committees, but Ora refused to let Pearl get ahead of her. Consequently, the Scotia church had more wax on its office floor and less dust on its hymnals than any other country church in Allamakee County.

On this August afternoon the heavy hot air carried organ chords out through the open windows of the church. Pearl was practicing the hymns for the coming Sunday, hymns of her choice. She played loudly, to drown Ora's arguments about the choice.

The dog, far above the church, heard the music and mildly enjoyed the sound.

In the big square gray house across from the church, Ora's youngest daughter heard the music, too. For Rhody, it was the all-clear signal.

# Chapter 2

RHODY came out onto the front porch, her cowboy boots clomping loudly. Because there was nobody in the house to yell at her not to, she let the screen door slam. She curled up on the porch swing and, in the secrecy of her lap, started to pry the wrapping off the bar of Switzer's licorice.

The licorice was her trophy. She'd had to hunt for it for half an hour today, after her mother left for the church. This time it had been hidden in Ora's second dresser drawer, under the corsets and the pink support hose. The contest had been going on all summer, ever since Rhody had discovered that her mother bought candy bars when she went for groceries on Thursday nights, and then hid them in her bedroom for her own pleasure. The candy seemed to be fair game to Rhody, since it came from the family grocery money, but she was beginning to wonder how long it would be before her mother caught on and whaled her.

She ate the licorice slowly, peeling off one cord at a time. It lasted about twice as long that way. She could put off, for that much longer, the thing she was gathering her courage to do. It was probably one of her stupidest ideas, but she knew she was going to try it anyhow. Just as soon as the candy was finished.

The front yard was a dark tangle of huge old lilacs, snowball bushes, and an ancient pine that towered over the house. But from one spot in the arc of the porch swing Rhody could see through the bushes and into the church across the road. She could see one hip of Aunt Pearl sitting at the organ, and from time to time she could see her mother dusting the pulpit. She felt a sudden weight of regret at what she was going to do, and it surprised her.

She was hot. Her jeans and boots held in her own heat, and her dark bangs stuck to the sweat on her face. The press of the air, and her uneasiness about her plan, made the thought of walking from the porch to Emil's barn a heavy prospect.

But the licorice was gone.

Walking stiffly because of the boots, she went out into the sun's glare, up the edge of the road past the empty post office, past Melkies' store, across Emil's yard, and around his house toward the barn. The sound of his power saw led her.

At the barn lot fence she paused, stood on the bottom board, and spoke to the two rust-black workhorses who stood waiting to die. They were among the small circle of Rhody's friends.

Emil came to the shop door and stood squinting into the sun. He resembled a coat hanger, with his small bald head, his curved shoulders from which his overalls seemed to hang empty of life. In one hand he held a chair rocker.

"What are you up to today?" he asked, as he always did.

"No good, that's for sure. What are you making?"

She followed him inside the cluttered little shop room and sat on her upended grapefruit crate.

Emil held up two pieces of the broken rocker from which he had drawn a pattern on new wood. "Folks think it's easy fixing one of these things. They don't stop to figure how wide a piece you need, for the curve. And the grain's got to go the right way or it'll break again. And then they expect me to do it for nothing." He worked the board into the jigsaw and flipped on the switch.

Usually Rhody enjoyed the rare days when Emil was grouchy, so long as she herself remained in his favor. She hoped he would become such an old grump that no one but she would like him at all, and then he would be grateful to have her. But today, with such an important proposition to put to him, she would have preferred a better mood.

While she waited for him to quit sawing, she tried to plan the first words.

The saw's whine died. Emil said, "Got a letter from my daughter today. Said the kids was getting all excited about starting high school. Said this school they'll be going to has a swimming pool. Inside. Heated even. Ain't that the berries?"

Rhody disliked his grandchildren, on principle, but at least they made an opening for the subject she wanted to get to.

"You really enjoyed your kids when they were little, didn't you?"

" 'Course I did. They was all good kids. Not a throw-away in the litter. Look at that." He held up the new rocker alongside the taped-together broken one. "Mary was my favorite, I think. 'Course, you ain't supposed to have favorites, and the boys was good, too, but that Mary . . ."

Rhody clenched her fists between her knees and plunged in. "I was just thinking about something." She paused, hoping he would turn and give her his full attention, but when he went on working, fitting the rocker into the saw again, she said, "I was thinking—wouldn't you like to have another daughter?"

He laughed a harsh laugh. "Little too late for that, girlie, with me in my seventies and my wife in her grave eight years."

"No, I was thinking about—me."

He turned then and glanced down at her over his shoulder. "What are you talking about?"

"Well"—she used her most logical voice—"look at it this way. My folks don't really want me over there. They were tired of having kids by the time I came along. You like me better than they do, and I like you better than them, and you're always talking about how lonesome you get, living here alone. And besides I could help you a lot. I can cook, kind of, and I could take care of the horses for you. And anything else you wanted me to do."

He turned back to his saw but not before Rhody saw the corners of his mouth twitching.

She knew, then, that it wasn't going to work.

"You sure get some crazy ideas sometimes, Rhody French. They must come from your dad's side of the family. Ora never had a silly notion in her life, and I've known her since the day she was born."

"I know. You told me a hundred times. *Why* is it a silly notion? It makes sense to me."

"Oh, go on, girl. Talk about something sensible. Did I tell you the grandkids are coming over Labor Day weekend?"

"I don't want to hear about your old grandchildren," Rhody snapped. She stood up and went outside to talk to Bonnie. The horse's great purple-shaded eye was a pool of sympathy.

Rhody shouted, "I'm going to ride Bonnie home, okay?"

Emil came out, snapped a lead rope onto the horse's halter, and led her out into the yard. Rhody reached high over her head for a handful of mane, while Emil grasped her booted ankle and heaved her up onto Bonnie's back. For a moment the man's hand remained tight around her leg.

"Hey, missy," he said, squinting at her, "you come again when you can stay longer, hear?"

She thumped him lightly on his bald spot

with the end of the lead rope, but there was no warmth in the familiar routine.

By kicking as hard as she could without losing her balance, she drummed Bonnie into a heavy trot. Around the house they jogged, past Melkies' store. At the post office she slowed Bonnie to a walk, to make the ride last longer. She could see her mother and Aunt Pearl on the church steps, but she turned her head away from them.

Far up on the bluff, near the top, there was something that wasn't usually there, a blot of black near one of the boulders. But before her eyes could find it for sure, the trees blocked her vision, and then she was home.

She slid off onto the tractor tire that held her outgrown sandpile. With a good hard hug around the mare's neck, Rhody knotted the lead rope up out of the way and turned her loose. Bonnie ambled toward home, pausing for bites of dusty grass along the way.

As she watched the mare, Rhody tore a leaf from a lilac bush and made a crisp, juicy fold in it. Her fingers folded the leaf again and again and, when it was ruined, flung it down. She felt hollow.

He hadn't even taken her idea seriously enough to argue about it. He didn't want her, either.

"Okay for you, Emil Bierbaum. You're just a dumb old man, anyway."

She sniffed loudly and fed her fury until it drove away the burning in the bridge of her nose. And she made a vow never to go visit Emil again. Not until he came and begged her.

# Chapter 3

THEY were still at the supper table—Rhody, her father, and her mother—when Aunt Pearl and Uncle Jack backed their car across the road into Frenches' lane and honked. Rhody's father went to the door, shouted, "Come on in and have dessert," and settled back into his chair.

Verden French was a small-boned man, shorter than his wife. He was quick and bright and vain about his flat stomach. All the women in Bill's Bar in nearby Lansing liked him, and he liked them. He was generally cheerful, but he had a slippery way of being somewhere else whenever there was anything that needed doing.

"Rhody, get plates," Ora said. Rhody reached down two more cake plates and cups and saucers.

Uncle Jack filled the whole kitchen with his quiet good humor. Without saying anything at all, he seemed to overshadow Pearl's steady small complaints. Rhody loved him. He was very tall and thin, and his hair waved straight back from his face in neat crinkles.

"Hi, Skeeziks," he said as he poked Rhody and then straddled his chair.

Pearl sat down, too, but she fussed a little at the delay.

"We better not sit around all evening if we want to get there before dark," she said. But she dug into the cake and sugared her coffee with as much gusto as her husband.

"No hurry," Ora said. "Ma's not going anywhere." She ignored Pearl's disapproving look and turned to Rhody. "You coming with us? You haven't seen Grandma for a long time."

Rhody had a strong dislike for the weekly

trips to the nursing home. She could never think of anything to say to the old woman who was her grandmother, and she always ended up sitting on the ridges of the radiator staring out the window while the rest of them talked.

"I'd rather stay home."

Pearl frowned, and Rhody relaxed. If Aunt Pearl was going to disapprove of her, her mother would almost certainly take her side.

Ora saw the frown, too. Quickly she said, "Well, I guess it isn't much for a kid, being in that old place."

Verden, who didn't want to go either, took his cue. "I'll stay home and watch the kid. You all go along. We'll entertain each other."

*Sure* we will, Rhody thought. We'll entertain each other by you going into town for a few beers. Oh well, that's still better than me having to go with them to see Grandma.

Half an hour after the two women and Uncle Jack had left, Verden ambled through the kitchen, where Rhody was putting away the last of the supper dishes. His hands were patting vaguely at his shirt pockets.

"Ran out of pipe tobacco," he said. "Guess I'll–"

"Go into town and get some." Rhody finished the sentence with him. "That's okay. You don't need to watch me."

He gave her a quick guilty hug and left.

She tried to enjoy the luxury of being alone in the house, but tonight her spirit was somewhere else. She switched off the kitchen light and wandered around the living room, turning the television on and off again, sitting for a few minutes in the window seat of the round tower in the corner of the room. The upstairs part of the tower was in her bedroom. She had had to wait until the last of her older brothers and sisters left home before she could have the tower room since it was, naturally, the pick of the bedrooms.

Tonight, for the first time in a long time, she wished some of them were still at home. She remembered evenings like this one, summer evenings with the breeze and the insect noises coming in through the tower windows. She used to curl up in the tower and watch the older kids and their friends while they shoved each other off the piano bench and played crazy duets and flirted with each other. And later, upstairs, if the girls were in a good mood, they'd let her come in their room and watch them learning how to shave their legs or put on eye makeup. Once they had put one of their bras on Rhody and filled it with rolled-up socks and sent her downstairs to shock the folks. But she was only six then and hadn't had enough rib even to keep the socks in the cups.

The house seemed so empty tonight.

She went over to the piano to play "Chopsticks," but she couldn't remember which two notes to start on, and it came out sounding awful.

She went outside. Beyond the jungle blackness of the front yard her world was lit by a nearly full moon. She placed herself in the middle of the road, one foot on either side of the center crack, and held out her arms to stop imaginary traffic. She turned a half-circle with just the top of her body and let the traffic go by. Then, with her feet still in place, she kept turning until her legs twisted and collapsed.

There were lights from only two other houses in Scotia besides her own—Melkies' back room and Emil's kitchen.

Rhody would have liked to go down to

Emil's, to sit on his back steps with him for a while, but she was still mad at him from this afternoon, so that was out.

With a sudden surge of life, she picked herself up, flapped her whole body as though she were a horse rolling in the dust, and ran as hard as she could up the road. She made it an all-out effort, arms tensed tight, head down, legs moving as fast as they could and then one notch faster. It felt good until the scratching began in her chest and she had to stop and breathe.

She was in front of her favorite of all the empty houses in Scotia. It was two houses spliced together, a white frame one across the front, and an older stone house behind it. It stood just beyond the church cemetery and had been used for years as the parsonage. But for the past several years the church had only an every-other-Sunday visiting minister, and the house had stood empty, as much Rhody's as anyone's.

Her breath was whistling in and out from the running; her chest was heavy, and her heart pounded with the effort of its pumping. One of Rhody's biggest fears was that her parents would find out that she wheezed and make her go to the doctor. There would undoubtedly be shots, or maybe an operation of some kind. She was sickly afraid of anything going into her skin, like needles. But so far she had managed not to have to wheeze when her folks were around, and out here alone she didn't mind it. It always broke up and went away in a few minutes.

She swam through the head-high weeds around the double house and pulled open the cellar door in the back. Rhody knew every beam, every crate and table stored in the basement, but there was enough tantalizing fear in her to make her leave the door open in case she needed to get out of there fast.

This was the stone part of the house. The basement room was huge. Chilly. Just enough moonlight came through the windows to blacken most of the room with velvet shadows.

Rhody felt her way toward her cave, the alcove under the steps leading upstairs. The entire alcove was filled with a leather fainting couch, long and flat but curving up at one end to form an arm or a pillow, depending on whether you were sitting or lying down.

With one swipe at the dusty leather, Rhody lay down. She closed her eyes. This was her house. She was old. Not *old* old, but old enough to be beyond the reach of doctors' needles and schools and lonesomeness.

Her mind grew furry. The couch seemed to sway as she started the downward spiral of sleep. Suddenly she jerked and screamed a small scream. A dark animal shape was close beside her, breathing on her, touching her face with its wet nose.

# Chapter 4

THE ANIMAL jumped when she screamed but then stood, its tail wagging gently.

Rhody melted. Her heart still hammered, but only from the suddenness of her awakening. She held out her hand.

"Hi."

The dog came close again and smelled her breath. Her hand moved in long, slow, hard strokes over his skull, his neck and shoulders and ribs. Abruptly he sat and hooked his paw over her arm, pulling it toward him.

"Hey, you're some dog," she said, with soft wonder. "Where did you come from? Did you come to be my dog because you knew I was lonesome? I bet you did. I bet I dreamed you up and you came."

The dog inched closer.

"My name is Rhody French. How do you do?"

She shook his paw and dropped it, but the dog hooked it over her arm and pulled her hand close again.

"Do you want to come *up?*" She patted the couch, and without hesitation the dog leaped up beside her. When he stretched out with his head in her lap, he covered almost the entire couch. Rhody shifted to give him more room.

"Wow, you really are big. I love big dogs."

While her stub-nailed fingers worked at a knot of cockleburs behind his ear, she talked on. She told him about her house, her family.

"I've got three brothers and three sisters. John's twenty-nine, lives in California, works for a computer company, has three kids. Verden Junior's twenty-six. He's in the Air Force. Sarah's the next one. She lives in Waterloo, has a dumb husband and two very bratty kids. Jerry's twenty-one, and he's out in California with John till he decides what he wants to do. Jane and Gretchen live in an apartment in Dubuque and work in offices, but Gretchen's going to college at night. And then I came along. They really didn't want any more kids, and you can't blame them, after six."

The dog pushed his head deeper into her stomach and thrashed his tail once. He sighed a long sigh.

Rhody sat still for as long as she could, but gradually her eyes insisted on going out of focus and her head would not stay where it belonged. Carefully she shifted until she was lying down against the pillowed arm of the couch, with the dog's head atop her hip. She dozed, smiling.

In less than an hour she woke, cramped and groggy and disconnected from reality. The dog was warm against her legs.

"Come on. Let's go home." She smoothed back his ears. "They might not know it yet, but we've got a new dog in the family. I'm going to keep you forever. No matter what."

Near the basement door was a coil of clothesline rope. She knew exactly where it was because she had tossed it there herself a few days ago, after several unsuccessful attempts to make a workable lasso out of it. She groped through the cluttered dark until she found it.

"Now you can't get away," she whispered as she knotted the rope around the dog's neck. He wagged and leaned against her.

They hopped up the cellar steps and into the moon-spattered yard. The dog moved at her side, bumping softly against her leg every few steps. Down the middle of the road they went, faster, jogging, running, the dog cantering close to her knee, his tongue lolling from the corner of his mouth. Rhody was as light now as she had been heavy a few hours ago. Even her wheezing was lighter. Shifts and adjustments were made in the back of her mind. Emil was forgiven, Aunt Pearl was forgotten, Ora was simply Mother again, a figure to be gotten around but not particularly noticed.

The dog was everything.

He followed her willingly across the porch as far as the dining room door, but he refused to step inside the house. He tested the linoleum with one foot, found it dangerous, and balked.

"Come on. Don't be so silly."

The house was dark except for the light in her parents' bedroom.

"Where have you been?" Ora bellowed.

"Nowhere. Just out," Rhody answered, hoping that would satisfy her mother for the time being. To the dog she whispered, "It's all right, boy. Come on. You have to come in. You're going to sleep in my room with me. Even on the bed if you want to. Come on now."

He lowered his head, stiffened his spine, and threw his weight back against the pull of the rope. It tightened, and he gagged.

"You come in, right now," Rhody commanded. She hauled him halfway through the door but had to let up for fear of choking him. His body went rigid. He clenched his toes against the slick floor. Terrified, he flung himself backward, back to the safety of the porch.

All of the air went out of Rhody.

"Okay. You win. Look, here. I'll tie you to the porch railing for tonight. You can get under the porch a ways if you want, or you can sleep right here. I'll be down first thing in the morning, okay? I love you."

She wrapped her arms around him, buried her face in his neck. It felt so good to have something to hug that her throat swelled from wanting to cry.

The dog listened to the receding footsteps, through the house, up the stairs, toward the front of the house again at a higher level. Boots were dropped. Bedsprings creaked.

He lay down against the porch railing. It pressed uncomfortably against his spine. He shifted to a spot under the swing. It wasn't right either. He went down the steps and started across the yard, but the rope stopped him several feet short of the inviting cave of bare dirt under the lilac bush.

The rope angered him. He had been tied only a few times in his life, and always the feeling of confinement was intolerable to him.

He sat down and began to gnaw the rope.

# Chapter 5

IT WAS gray and dripping dawn when Rhody moused down the stairs and across the dining room. She wore short pajamas made from Gretchen's hand-me-downs, and her hair spiked out at odd angles.

She opened the screen door and whispered, "Here I–"

The chewed end of the rope curled across the sidewalk.

"Oh, no!"

As she stared at the rope, her mind saw the dog working at it with his teeth, working patiently through the night, working to get away from her.

*He* didn't like her either. Not her mother, nor Emil, nor Aunt Pearl, and now not even the dog. Whatever it was about her that was so bad, the dog sensed it, too. He had chewed and chewed on the rope just to get away from her.

She clenched her small jaw and stumped back into the house. "I'm going to find you, and I'm going to keep you and *make* you love me."

While she pulled on her jeans and boots and shirt, she thought. It rained in the night, so maybe he made footprints. I'll follow him, and I'll keep on following him till I find him. I'll take a sandwich, maybe an orange. Then I can keep looking all day. First I'll cover all the territory from here to the new highway, and from the bluff to the creek. Then...

In the kitchen Ora stood in her nightgown, staring with unfocused eyes out the sink window while she ran water into the coffeepot. Her face bore red creases from her pillow.

"What you doing up so early?" she asked as Rhody began fishing in the bread box.

"I'm going out. I'll take my breakfast with me."

Ora made a sound that might have been approval, disapproval, or disinterest, as she scooped coffee grounds into the pot's basket.

Rhody put the orange and a hastily made sugar sandwich into a plastic sack Ora kept for mushroom hunting in the spring. The sack had drawstrings, which Rhody tied through her belt loops so that both hands would be free for whatever climbing or scrambling might be necessary.

"Be back later."

Outdoors was freedom and misty sunshine. The front yard offered no paw prints, no hint as to which way the dog might have gone. Rhody went to the middle of the road and revolved as slowly as if she were getting a hem pinned, while her eyes searched every yard, every shadow, every surface, they could reach.

"Eenie meenie minie moe, if I were a dog, which way would I go?"

Start at the starting place. She made a quick

tour of her own yard—under porches, around peonies, tire swing, sandpile, vegetable garden, woodshed, pump house. Then out the back gate that had no fence to it. Around and in and out of all the buildings—garage; big chicken house; little chicken house with weeds pushing up through its floorboards; barn, both the basement level where the cows were and the upper level where the hay and kittens were; hog house; corncrib; machine shed. She picked her way through the junk area behind the machine shed where old fence posts and a rusted harrow made winter homes for rats and rabbits. She climbed the lane gate and walked the length of the calf pasture, scanning the slope for a bit of movement, a black shadow.

She circled back along the edge of the oat field. There was no use looking in the cornfield. The corn was well above her head. It would be impossible to see a dog in there.

"Okay, so he's not on our place."

She cut across the backyard, across the weed-grown area behind the old post office. Some of the weeds were stinging nettles, and she moved cautiously through them just in case it was true, what Uncle Jack always said, that they wouldn't sting you if you held your breath. It didn't make sense to her, but she did it anyway.

"Phew," she gasped, emerging from the head-high weeds into Mrs. Melkie's backyard.

The dog lay against the back step, shredding a bologna wrapper. Rhody stopped. "You're here," she breathed, filling herself with the sight of him.

He looked up from the bologna wrapper. His tail banged against the garbage can as he rose and ambled toward her. He grinned and came up into her arms.

The door opened. "Where'd that thing come from?" Mrs. Melkie asked. Her squatty form was clothed, as usual, in a flowered blouse, ballooning slacks, white socks, and high-heeled sandals. She lived alone in the two rooms behind the store, sold dusty groceries and worked the gas pumps, and waited for her husband to come home. He had disappeared eleven years ago.

Rhody gripped the dog's rope. "He's my new dog. How do you like him? Isn't he beautiful?"

Mrs. Melkie sniffed. "If that's your dog, you keep him out of my garbage can, hear?" She faded back into the dimness behind her.

"She's a witchy old thing," Rhody whispered. "We don't have to pay any attention to her."

The dog reared to his full height and draped his front paws over Rhody's shoulders.

"You weren't really trying to get away from me, were you?" she murmured.

He pressed his head down across her shoulder, against her neck. For a long moment they stood that way while all of Rhody's darkness washed up and out of her.

She beat a gay rhythm against his ribs.

"Come on. I've got to show you to Emil."

They made the rounds of Scotia. Emil stroked the dog's head and said he looked like some kind of a hunting dog, and he sure was nice. Aunt Pearl said that's nice, but don't let him in the house, the parakeet's loose. Uncle Jack was genuinely enthusiastic. He endeared himself to Rhody by saying he reckoned the dog didn't belong to anybody around Scotia, so he was probably a stray and might as well belong to Rhody as anybody. With a keen warm look he added, "I think you've been kinda needing a friend here lately, Skeeziks."

Ora was the scary one. Rhody filled her lungs with breath before she led the dog across the road and around to the backyard. Ora was picking green beans.

"Look at my new dog, Mom. I found him last night and he followed me home and he was still here this morning. So I can keep him, can't I? He's a real nice dog."

Ora studied the dog from her squatting position between beans and tomato plants.

"Found him, huh?"

"Yeah. He's real thin, so I know he doesn't belong to anybody."

Ora raised her eyebrows.

Quickly Rhody said, "You always let the older kids have all the pets they wanted, when they were little. Dogs and rabbits, and a pony that time. I never even asked for a pony. All I want is this dog, and if you say I can't have him, it's no fair."

Ora opened her mouth to argue, but closed it again. The other kids had had pets. Endless strings of them. This time Rhody was right. "Oh, I don't care. Ask your dad." She went back to her beans.

Rhody galloped away toward the barn with the dog in step beside her. "I get to keep you, I get to keep you," she sang. She understood that the formality of asking her father's permission was just so he wouldn't feel left out of things.

Verden was in the lower level of the barn, rubbing Udder Balm into the caked teats of one of the milk cows. Rhody knew better than to go in and risk disturbing the cow, so she held the dog in the doorway and called, "Daddy, lookit. I got a new dog. I found him last night, and Mom said I can keep him if you say so. Okay?"

Verden glanced over his shoulder at her. "As long as he don't bother the stock. Scoot off now."

Up over the rock-terraced bank they climbed, around the side of the barn to the upper level. Rhody heaved back one of the giant doors and led the dog inside.

"Watch where you step, now. There's feed-chute holes along there. I want to show you my special place."

She led him to the farthest corner of the barn, where the sunlight filtered only dimly through the dust and cobwebs. Stacks of hay bales were left here from last year's cutting—mammoth building blocks piled as high as twenty feet in some places. Early in the summer Rhody had spent two days dragging and shifting the bales, arranging them into walls and partitions for her house. Broken bales provided a foot-thick cushion that was both floor and furniture. Here, in the smallest and most deeply hidden of her three rooms, she let go of the dog's rope and sprawled on the floor. He dropped beside her.

"Look. We've got breakfast." She untied the mushroom sack and divided the food, sugar sandwich for him, orange for her.

"I thought of a name for you in the night last night. Royal. That's going to be your name. Okay?"

He wolfed the sandwich. When it was gone, he hooked his paw over her arm and pulled her hand into scratching position.

"Royal," she sighed and settled back into the hay. "My own dog, forever."

# Chapter 6

WHEN Ora called lunch, Rhody tried again to lead the dog into the house. It was the back door this time, and the kitchen floor, but the results were the same —lowered head, braced feet, absolute refusal to step on the linoleum.

"Stupid dog," Ora said.

"Mother!"

Ora swooped down on Royal, picked him up as if he were a calf, and dumped him in the center of the kitchen.

"Mom, don't."

Eyes wide with fear, the dog clattered on clenched toes out the door and down the steps. When Rhody caught up with him, he was standing near the tire swing, panting and trembling.

"That's all right, Royal. That's okay," Rhody murmured, pressing his neck against her legs. "You don't have to come in the house, ever. Nobody's going to make you, if it scares you that much. Just come back to the porch with me."

He followed her back to the porch steps.

"Mom, can I eat my lunch out here with him?" Rhody called. She tied his short rope to the handle of the cistern pump, and the dog lay down.

Ora brought out a plate of cold ham and baked beans and a glass of milk. She looked at the dog, then at her daughter, and finally said, "You planning to stay tied to that dog for the rest of your life?"

"He only has to be tied up till he knows this is his home. It won't take long. Probably by tonight he'll be settled down."

That afternoon Uncle Jack brought over a stout leather collar and chain leash, left from a farm dog that had been run over by a tractor a few years before. When she went in for supper, Rhody chained Royal to the cistern pump. Halfway through the meal she looked out the window and saw him backing out of the collar. She ran outside, caught him, buckled the collar tighter. It took him until dessert to back out of it.

She caught him again, tied him again, and brought her ice cream out to the back steps where she could keep him company. He settled down, then, to the pan of food Rhody had served him before she went in to her own dinner.

Ora and Verden came out to sit above Rhody on the porch.

"What you going to do about him tonight?" Ora asked. "You can't get him in the house, and you can't tie him up. I think you ought to turn loose of him. If he wants to stay, he will, and if he don't, he won't."

"Oh, Mom."

It was one of those times when her mother's dense failure to understand was a physical pain in Rhody.

"Well, don't 'Oh, Mom' me. Tell me. What *are* you going to do about him?"

Rhody thought.

"I'll sleep in the tent, for tonight anyway. Probably by tomorrow he'll be okay."

Ora blew out noisily through her lips.

The tent was an invention of Rhody's older brothers. It was made of two patchwork quilts fastened together over the clothesline. The floor was a piece of canvas dug out of the cluttered recesses of the barn, and the end flaps were huge discarded bath towels. The bed was four more quilts piled atop one another for softness.

It took Rhody most of the rest of the evening to assemble it all, but when she was finally stretched out on the quilts, with her parents out of sight in the house and no light but the stars and the lightning bugs, she sighed a huge sigh of peace. Royal lay beside her. He was tied to her ankle just in case he got restless in the night, but he seemed to be entirely content.

"This was a pretty good idea," she told him. "Heck, we could sleep out here all the rest of the summer if we want to. Except when it rains. What do you think about that?"

His tail struck the canvas.

# Chapter 7

FOR THE next two weeks the tent stayed up, except for washdays when Ora needed the clothesline. The nights were hot, airless. Rhody's muscles became stiff and her stomach was strung with chigger bites, but Royal remained.

Gradually Rhody began leaving him unleashed during the day, while she was outdoors with him. He seemed contented enough, so she went back to eating her meals in the kitchen. The dog stayed on the back porch.

Still, she didn't quite trust him not to run away in the night, and so the tent stayed up.

One morning Pearl said to Ora, "How long are you going to let that child sleep outdoors like that?"

Ora, Verden, and Rhody were eating breakfast. Pearl, who had not only eaten her breakfast already but had also washed the dishes and dusted three rooms of her house, was just drinking coffee.

"Till she molds, if she wants to," Ora said. "Verden, pass the butter."

Rhody looked from her aunt to her mother as she raised her honey-dripping toast toward her mouth. She was not particularly worried, though. Whenever Pearl criticized Rhody, Ora's automatic reaction was to defend her daughter. Sometimes Rhody felt as though the only kind words her mother ever gave her were said to anger Pearl.

"Well," Pearl said doubtfully, "if she were a daughter of mine—"

"Oh, bull-tickie, Pearl. What on earth could be wrong with Rhody sleeping out in the tent if she feels like it? It's cooler out there than in that upstairs bedroom, and if she doesn't mind the chiggers and mosquitoes, why should you care?"

"It's not the chiggers I'd be worried about if she were a daughter of mine," Pearl said heavily.

Rhody interrupted. "I wish you'd quit saying 'she' all the time, like I wasn't even in the room."

Both women turned and frowned down at her. She picked up another piece of toast and dipped her knife into the honey.

Ora turned her attention back to Pearl. "And just what did you mean by that last remark?"

"You know very well what I mean. She's a girl. You can't tell who might be wandering around. Bums, drunks, you can't tell. She could get killed, or worse, before you'd hear a thing, with your bedroom on the other side of the house."

Ora's laughter exploded through the kitchen, and even Verden smiled down into his coffee cup.

"Bums and drunks," Ora hooted. "Pearl, when have you ever seen a bum, or any kind of a stranger for that matter, come through here on foot at night? And you've lived right here on this spot all your fifty-six years."

"Well—"

"Well, nothing. We aren't even anywhere near a railroad track, or a highway big enough to have hitchhikers. Ain't nobody around here but what we've known them all our lives, and ain't nobody going to hurt that kid."

"Besides," Rhody said, "you're all forgetting one thing. I've got Royal for protection. If anybody ever came near me, he'd kill them."

Ora snorted. "That dog can't even walk across a floor without having a heart attack. I don't think I'd want to depend on his bravery for any great amount of protection."

Verden said, "I don't know, Orie. You can't ever tell about a dog. They get attached to a person, and they'll surprise you sometimes. That old Laddie we had when I was a kid, he went after that bull—you remember when that Angus bull went crazy that time and cornered Uncle John. Old Laddie was generally kind of timid around the cattle, but that time he went right after that bull, bit him on the nose and got the bull to chasing him instead of Uncle John. Boy, if Uncle John didn't load up his gun and blow that bull's brains from here to—"

"We're at the table," Pearl reminded him.

Verden looked her up and down. "So what? You're not eating anything, and the rest of us can take it."

Ora turned to Rhody. "You better hop and get cleaned up. We'll be ready to go just as quick as I clear off the table."

Rhody had been stiffening against the inevitable argument all through breakfast. "I don't want to go. I told you clear last week I'd rather stay home. You can go without me."

Verden's head came up sharply. "You don't want to go to Sweet Corn Days? I never heard of a kid that didn't want to go to a parade. And the midway and the beard contest and tractor pull, not to mention all that food. What's the matter with you?"

"Nothing's the matter with me. I just would rather stay home. I don't *have* to go, do I? You guys will have more fun without me."

"But why don't you want to?" Verden persisted. "It'll be lots of fun. What have you got to do around here that's more important than going to Sweet Corn Days?"

"Nothing."

Pearl cleared her throat. "If she was a daughter of mine–"

"Oh, Pearl, shut up," Ora snapped. "If you'd wanted kids so bad, why didn't you have them? Rhody doesn't want to go off and leave the dog. That's all that's the matter with her."

Pearl looked down at Rhody. "You still having trouble with that dog running away? If he wants to go so bad, why don't you let him? It's mean to keep a dog tied up against his will, dear."

Rhody shook her head furiously but didn't trust her voice.

"Oh, leave her alone," Ora said. "She don't have to go if she don't want to. If she wants to miss out on the fun, it's no skin off my nose."

# Chapter 8

RHODY and Royal stayed in the barn, in the inner room of the hay-bale house, until the car clattered out the lane and hummed away. She wouldn't have admitted it to anyone, but now that they were gone, she couldn't help thinking about the parade she'd be missing, and the midway. And the cotton candy. Sweet Corn Days was about the only time all year that she could get cotton candy. She tried not to think about wrapping her tongue around a grainy strand of the stuff.

"Listen, Royal, you and I are going to do something good today. By ourselves. What would you like to do?"

He leaned against her and looked up, tongue dripping from the corner of his mouth. His look was bright and warm, and when she smiled down at him, he wrapped his paw around her wrist.

"I know what. You haven't seen my secret place yet. Let's go up there."

She stopped in the kitchen long enough to fill the plastic pouch with cheese and a handful of chocolate-chip cookies, and then they were off.

First they went to Emil's.

"Could I ride Bonnie for a while, Emil? Royal and I are going up on the bluff, and it's too hot to walk all that way." She stood on one foot, squinting up into Emil's face.

"Oh, I reckon. But you be careful with her, now, and don't get her all sweaty."

"I know better than that."

The mare was bridled, an old patched work bridle with reins made from braided baling twine, and Rhody was boosted up.

"Thanks, Emil. Come on, boy. Let's go."

They went down an overgrown track behind the house where she first found Royal. The track had been a timber road at one time, and it climbed, sideways, up the bluff at its gentlest slope. Horseweed and wild blackberries filled the track, but Rhody, high on Bonnie's back, could tuck her feet up above them, and Royal didn't seem to mind leaping through them.

On top of the bluff the trees were so large and so close that they shaded out most of the undergrowth. The going was easier here. Bonnie's hooves shuffled through a gray-brown carpet of dead leaves.

They moved along the ridge of the bluff for nearly a mile, sometimes on the faint old timber road, sometimes losing it. Once Rhody slid from Bonnie's back to hold down a sagging wire fence for the horse to step over. Then she had to lead Bonnie for several minutes before she found a rock to stand on, so she could reach the horse's back again. Royal moved happily, nose down, ranging from side to side but never very far away.

The trees thinned out, and the sun came

through to a small grassy meadow. At the edge of it Rhody halted Bonnie and called to Royal.

"See over there?" She pointed to a place in the middle of the meadow, where the ground rose about three feet in a broad odd-shaped mound.

"It's hard to see it from here," Rhody explained to the dog, "but if you look at it right, you can see it's a bird. A dove, I call it, but I really don't know what kind of a bird. See, that's the head over there, where that bush is growing out of it, and the wings go across that way, and this is the tail, pointing over this way. It's thirty feet long and fifty feet from wing tip to wing tip. I measured it one time by walking it off, like my dad does when he's fencing."

The dog stood close beside her, but his eyes were on the grassy mound.

"You know who built it? The Indians. A thousand years ago! There's somebody buried inside it. My dad took me over to Effigy Mounds Park one time, and we saw the Indian mounds over there. They were kind of like this one, but not as good. And I didn't tell the park guys about this mound. It's mine. I'm the only one that knows about it."

She tied Bonnie to a tree and climbed the mound. At the place where the bird's heart would be, she lay down on the grass. Royal flopped beside her, panting.

She was just getting into a lovely daydream when voices brought her upright, heart pounding. Sticks crackled in the timber. Suddenly there were people in the meadow—a man, two women, and a girl who appeared to be a college student. They carried canvas packs and short-handled shovels.

Royal rose to his feet. With his eyes steady on the intruders, he lowered his head, growled softly, and moved to a spot between Rhody and the strangers.

Rhody stared at him. A ripple of delight washed through her. He was protecting her. That meant he loved her.

The intruders saw Rhody and the dog and stopped talking among themselves.

"Hi," one woman called. She looked familiar, someone seen in town at the Super Value or at Ward's, but not really known.

The man called, "Hot enough for you today?"

"Yes."

Royal's tail moved in a gentle arc then, and he relaxed against Rhody. The two of them sat and watched for several minutes while the man staked off a five-by-five-foot plot and the women, in jeans and old shirts, began the careful removal of the top inch of soil within the plot.

Rhody and the dog moved closer to the diggers.

"What are you doing?" she asked in spite of herself.

The college girl answered. "Digging for Indian relics, for the county museum. Arrowheads, pottery shards, things like that."

"Oh. You're not going to dig up the bird mound, are you?"

All four of the diggers looked toward the mound. With the sun directly overhead and almost no shadows to outline it, the mound was hard to see. It looked, from the side, like nothing more than the bank of a long-dead stream, and for an instant Rhody thought she might have imagined the bird shape.

But the man said, "Not on your shinbone, miss. That's one of the best effigy mounds around this area. We don't want to destroy it."

"I didn't think anybody knew about it but me," Rhody said. The others smiled, and she felt foolish. "Well, come on, Royal. We better start for home."

He trotted close beside her on the way back to Bonnie. Rhody's hand rode on the dog's neck. She hoped the diggers were watching, admiring the picture her dog made, moving through the long grass with his head and tail high. She felt a lovely power, having Royal for her partner.

# Chapter 9

THAT night Rhody sat with her father, Uncle Jack, and Emil, on Emil's back steps. The men had spent the evening cutting down an old apple tree and working it up into stove lengths for Emil. Now they sat, legs outspread, arms on knees, face sweat wiped off onto their sleeves. They were entertained by the heat lightning, the fireflies, and the retelling of favorite stories.

Rhody and Royal sat a little ways away, on the cistern lid, where she could enjoy the talk without being part of the group. Her mood was still light from Royal's show of loyalty up on the Indian mound.

Emil was talking. "Old Charlie." He chuckled. "He was some old Charlie, all right. You remember that time he got so drunk down there by the church when they was having that funeral? And a couple of them guys from Volga decided they was going to play a trick on old Charlie. So after the funeral was over and the hearse driver was down having a beer, they loaded old Charlie in the back of the hearse and stuck a flower in his hand. He was kind of passed out, like. Well, anyway, then they started talking real loud about what a good guy old Charlie was before he died. Well, sir, old Charlie he woke up and he sat up in that hearse and he yelled, 'I ain't dead. Did you fellers think I was dead? And you didn't even call my sister?'"

The men laughed, and Rhody grinned.

"'And you didn't even call my sister,' old Charlie yells."

The sound of laughter was buried under a long roll of thunder.

"I don't believe that *is* heat lightning anymore," Uncle Jack said. "I believe we're going to get a little weather."

Verden looked over at Rhody. "You ain't sleeping in that tent tonight, girl. Not in the rain."

"I know it," she answered in a cool voice. There was nothing to worry about anymore. Royal had declared her his master. He had shown that he loved her. He wouldn't run away again.

But just to be sure, when they went home, she shut him in the barn. "You'll be fine in here tonight," she told him. "I'll see you in the morning."

But in the morning he was gone.

The heavy door was still shut. None of the windows were broken, but the barn was empty. Rhody stared into its cobwebbed emptiness, and everything inside her sank. Her eyes and nose smarted with tears of disappointment, of frustration, of hurt.

The battle wasn't over yet. He still wanted to get away from her.

But *why?* she raged silently. *Why* does

he keep on wanting to get away from me? I love him.

She threw all of her fury into rolling the huge door shut again, then set out to begin the search. Her jaw ached from being clenched so hard.

All day she looked and called, through all the backyards in Scotia, along the highway for three miles, and back again. Part of her mind was saying, Okay, good riddance then, if that's the way you want it. But the lump of hurt grew bigger instead of smaller, and she knew she would have to keep looking until she found him.

Once, walking along the shoulder of the highway, she saw something large and dark lying beside the road. Her stomach heaved, and her head grew light. But it was a deer, struck by a car and tossed aside. It wasn't Royal. Rhody went home planning tomorrow's hunt.

It was nearly dark when a car drove in the Frenches' lane. From the dining room window Rhody saw the car door open, saw a woman get out–and Royal!

She was across the porch before the screen door could slam. "Royal! You're okay! Oh, wow, did you ever give me a scare."

The woman who watched, smiling, was one of the diggers from the afternoon before. "I guess that answers my question," she said. "He showed up over at our place this afternoon, looking for a handout. I thought he looked like your dog, and I was pretty sure you were Verden and Ora's girl."

Rhody gripped his collar with both hands and looked up at the woman. "Yes, he's mine. He just likes to go exploring sometimes. Thank you very, very much for bringing him back."

The phone was ringing inside the house as the woman drove away, but Rhody hardly noticed it. She led Royal up onto the front porch, held the door open with her hip, and tried to pull him inside. She was determined to get him into the house so that, from now on, he would spend the nights shut safely in her room. Until he loved her a little more.

"Mom, Dad, *look*–"

She stopped, amazed. Her father and mother were standing close together by the telephone. Ora was hunched over so that her head could reach down to the level of Verden's shoulder. His arms were around her. Neither was crying, but both of their faces were red and oddly pulled out of shape.

Ora stared at Rhody, then said, "Honey, that was the nursing home. Your grandma just passed away."

# Chapter 10

FOR THE next two days Rhody and Royal were all but invisible in the confusion that filled the house. Older sisters and brothers began arriving with their families. There was little real grief. After all, Grandma Gunnarsson was eighty-seven, and she had been in bed for the past three years, since that last stroke.

"Well, it's a blessing," they said to one another. "She went without any pain, and she had a good long life. How's everything at your place?"

As had been the case for as long as Rhody could remember, the older kids—all adults now—greeted her, remarked on how big she was getting or how nice and brown she looked, and then turned back to each other. Their interests were over the top of her head.

She and Royal moved into the tent again, since her room was filled with relatives. That suited her fine.

On the morning of the third day, though, Ora focused for a moment on her youngest. "Rhody. Hop up right now and wash your hair. It looks awful. It'll just about have time to get dry before we have to leave for the service."

Rhody's hand tightened around her fork. "I don't really have to go to the funeral, do I?"

Everyone in the crowded kitchen was suddenly silent. Their faces turned toward her, surprised, some of them shocked.

"Not go!" Ora barked. "What do you mean, not go? To your own grandmother's funeral? What kind of girl are you, anyway?"

Rhody's face hardened. She had a pretty good idea of what kind of girl she was. For the past two days she had given no more than a few minutes' thought to her grandmother. She had tried. She had tried to remember her grandmother as a person, smiling and moving about the house, not as a dry little figure who lay in a room at the nursing home and complained that no one came to visit her. But it was hard to remember so long ago. Rhody knew that the person who had just died was her mother's mother, and that Ora was probably grieving. But still Rhody felt no sadness, only a private irritation that her own life was being disrupted—and a deep shame at her selfishness.

She tried to explain herself. "But it wouldn't make any difference to Grandma, whether I went or not. I didn't even hardly know her. And I have to stay here with Royal."

The disapproval only deepened. Rhody knew she was going to the funeral.

An hour later Rhody came out of the back door and sat down beside Royal. She was uncomfortable in dress and school shoes. Hair rollers teased the back of her neck.

"What are we going to do with you?" she asked, holding the dog's head between her hands. "I've got to put you someplace where you absolutely can't get out. If I lost you . . ."

The barn was out. The house was out. Rhody could just imagine the damage Royal could do, shut in the house alone for three hours. Where else? Machine shed—corncrib—chicken house—a resourceful dog could get out of any of them. Garage—maybe.

"I tell you what. I'll tie you up inside the garage. That should be double safe."

It was a narrow, leaning garage, dirt-floored, with just one window, high up in the back. In the far corner a workbench stood camouflaged by oil cans, bits of rope and leather, and old jars of rusted nails and bolts. Hanging from a nail was a length of stout chain with an escape-proof bull clasp on one end. Rhody fastened the chain to one leg of the workbench and to Royal's collar. Then she brought him a pan of water and bent down for one last hug.

"I hate to shut you in here, but it's your own fault. If you'd just quit running away! I'll be back as soon as I can, I promise. And I'll take you for a long walk before supper, to make up for putting you in here, okay?"

Quickly she backed out of the garage and pulled the doors shut. A long whine came from inside. She turned and ran to the car where her parents were waiting.

All the way to town, while her mother pulled the rollers out of her damp hair, Rhody tried not to hear the sound of Royal's whines. Bitterly she resented being pulled away from him, being forced to attend a funeral at which she was neither needed nor, in her opinion, wanted, being forced to leave her dog, who did need her and want her.

The funeral service seemed endless. The parlor of the funeral home was filled with flowers and sunshine and powdered old ladies in pastel dresses, who moved past Grandma Gunnarsson's casket and whispered how nice she looked. To Rhody, she looked like a life-sized doll whose skin looked as though it would feel funny if she dared to touch it. In an attempt to be a better person, Rhody forced herself to think about Grandma Gunnarsson and how sad it was that she was dead. But in spite of herself she simply couldn't make herself care. What was really important was Royal, chained inside that hot garage, maybe spilling his water and being thirsty, maybe thinking that she was mad at him and punishing him. He might be afraid she wasn't coming back. That was the bad thing, she thought while she sang "Nearer My God To Thee." You couldn't really make a dog understand.

At last it was over.

"I can hardly wait to get home," she whispered to her sister Gretchen as they climbed into the car.

"Oh, we're not going home yet," Gretchen said. "We have to go to the cemetery for the burial now."

"Oh, no." Rhody sagged.

It took an endless time for all of the cars to get lined up right. There was no breeze, and the back seat of the Frenches' car became a furnace to Rhody. Even dangling her arm out the window didn't help.

Finally they started off in slow procession behind the hearse. The fifteen-mile drive to Scotia took twice as long as usual, but finally they pulled into the churchyard, across the road from home.

While everyone was getting out of the cars

and moving slowly toward the spot at the top of the hill, where a large canopy covered an open grave, Rhody stared across the road at the garage where Royal waited. An odd feeling began to grow inside her, a feeling of something wrong, or out of place.

She hung back, pretending to tie her shoe at the back of the parked car. Her parents moved slowly up the hill away from her. Her sisters and brothers walked beside their husbands and wives and children, with a hand on an arm or across a shoulder. Rhody was forgotten.

Silently she moved along the row of cars—then behind the snowball bush. Then she made a soft-footed dash across the road.

Safe.

She pulled open the garage door.

"I'm back, Ro—"

The garage was empty.

The chain led up, up to the window and through it.

Rhody screamed.

# Chapter 11

SHE RAN around the garage. Royal hung against the weathered boards of the building, his feet a foot from the ground.

Rhody didn't know she was crying. She wasn't able to think, but her instincts took over. She wrapped her arms around the dog's ribs and lifted. The pressure of his self-made noose was eased, and his head fell back onto her shoulder.

It took a few minutes for the numbness of

shock to wear off. Then suddenly Rhody became aware that her hair was moving. Rasping puffs struck her cheek, her ear.

*He was alive.*

"Help me, somebody," she screamed.

But there was no one to hear. They were all beyond the reach of her voice, on top of the hill behind the church.

Rhody shifted a little and braced herself against the building. The dog was growing unbearably heavy, and yet there was no way of letting him go without returning his weight to his tortured neck.

Tears streamed down her face, but she clenched her jaw and tried to think. She found that by bracing one foot against the building she could support part of his weight on her leg.

She shouted again, and wondered how long it would be before anyone noticed that she wasn't at the burial. It could be a long time, she realized. Her parents would have other things on their minds.

The boards of the building were making painful ridges in her back. Her foot kept sliding down. She began to be genuinely afraid she wouldn't be able to hold him, that her arms would give out so suddenly that his neck would be broken.

"Oh, somebody *please* hurry up and come." It was a sob, and a whispered prayer.

Then she heard the sound of cars starting, gravel rattling, voices. Her mother's voice, angry.

"Rhoda! Rhoda Marie French!"

"Help, Mama!" she screamed.

Suddenly Ora was there. "Oh, my God, girl. Is he alive?"

Ora's arms lifted the dog. "Run get your dad, and a knife. We'll have to cut this collar off."

Rhody ran.

Half an hour later Rhody and Ora stood beside the metal table in the veterinarian's office. Royal lay on his side on the table. His neck was bandaged, and a plastic tube stuck sickeningly out of his throat. His breath whistled in and out of the tube.

"That tube shouldn't have to be in for more than a day or so," the doctor said. "Just till the swelling goes down in that tissue around his windpipe and he can breathe normally. But in the meantime somebody's going to have to watch that tube night and day. If it gets blocked with anything, the dog's not going to be able to get any air."

Rhody said, "I'll watch it. Don't worry." She felt her mother's hand on her shoulder, and suddenly she gave in to the childish urge to lean on Ora, to feel herself supported by her mother's strength.

Rhody and Royal took up residence in a corner of the kitchen, on a bed of newspapers and gunnysacks. She watched to be sure nothing got in the way of the air tube. That night and the next day she fed Royal sips of warm milk and, later when he could swallow a little, a thin gruel of milk and dog food. He lay still, with his head in Rhody's lap, and moved only to take occasional painful laps of the milk.

The morning after the funeral all of the company left. The house became its old quiet self again, and except for mealtimes, Rhody and Royal were left alone.

She did a lot of thinking in those long quiet hours while her hand stroked Royal's side.

I almost killed him, she thought again and again. It was my fault for trying to make him stay when he didn't want to. But I don't understand. He acts like he loves me. He was going to protect me, that time up on the mound, and he's always real glad to see me when I come out of the house. So why's he keep trying to get away? She puzzled it over, through the long hours of the night when she was afraid to fall asleep for fear he would stop breathing.

An answer came, finally.

Maybe it's just that he needs to have his freedom, she reasoned. Maybe he's not like other dogs, that have to have masters. Maybe for some reason he has to *not* have one, or at least not be tied down to one home. Probably if he *could* stay with one person, he'd want it to be me, but he just can't.

It was almost dawn when her thinking reached that point. Her back hurt, and her seat was numb from sitting on the hard floor for so long, but she didn't want to move and wake Royal. She stared down at him, at his long satiny muzzle, his closed eyes that moved slightly from his dreaming, the long black body that stretched away to the corner of the stove.

Rhody knew there was a decision, a big one, that had to be made. There could be no more tying Royal up or shutting him in or forcing him to stay. And yet something inside her would not allow Rhody to let go of him. He filled a large and aching need, and all of her instincts told her to hang onto him.

The minutes ticked past while Rhody fought with the problem. The sky outside the window became gray, then green-white, then pale blue. Suddenly Rhody smiled.

"Don't you worry, Royal. We're going to stay together—your way."

She slid lower, readjusted her legs, and finally slept.

# Chapter 12

TWO DAYS later Royal was nearly back to normal. The swelling in his neck was entirely gone, the breathing tube removed, and the small wound closed with a stitch. He could eat without pain, and he moved around the yard sniffing and wagging and renewing his acquaintance with life.

After supper Rhody put up the tent. As she was carrying the blankets out the back door, Ora said, "We're going over across for a while, Rhody."

Rhody stopped, shocked for an instant at her mother's callousness. But then she remembered that Ora didn't know this was Rhody's last night at home.

When Ora and Verden were gone, Rhody came back into the house and filled the plastic pouch with apples, a packet of graham crackers, half a package of bologna, and a handful of Oreo cookies. She got her waterproof jacket from the closet. Then, with a nervous glance through the dining room windows toward the house across the street, she wrote a brief note and propped it on the bread box.

Royal was standing below the back porch as she came out.

"Okay, friend, we'd better get going in case they come back early. You lead. We'll go wherever you want to."

The dog stood waving his tail gently.

"You have to lead," she insisted. "You're the one who has to be a stray. You just go wherever you'd go if I wasn't with you."

Together they walked out the lane. The dog paused beside the road. He sensed Rhody's hesitation. After an instant he turned left. She followed. He moved out more surely, and so did Rhody. Suddenly they were running with their heads up, their hearts swelling. If she wheezed, she didn't know it. Night magic carried them.

At the old parsonage they turned and began climbing the timber road, up the face of the bluff. The woods closed in around them, shutting off the moonlight. Rhody was thankful that the food pouch was tied around her waist. She needed both hands to fight her way through the underbrush and to hang onto Royal's back. He led her gently, but it was rough work pushing through the tangle of berry bushes that filled the ghost of a road.

After what seemed an endless climb, the road leveled off on the crest of the bluff and the bushes thinned away.

"Ah . . ."

They were still without light, but now Rhody began to enjoy the feeling of being piloted by the dog. "I wouldn't even mind being blind," she told him, "if I had a good Seeing Eye dog like you."

Her logical mind had been deliberately

turned off. She did not allow herself to think about tomorrow, or the future after that. She had made a decision based on emotion and instinct, and she felt confident that somehow it would work out.

Royal had been a stray all his life. He managed to find food and shelter when he needed it. Somehow, in some way she hadn't yet thought through, Royal would take care of her, too. She had heard stories of dogs bringing food to other animals who were marooned or hurt, keeping them alive. Maybe he would do that for her. Or maybe they'd just travel around the country begging. Or she could offer to do some work to pay for their food, housework or something like that.

The impossibilities of the plan she stubbornly pushed aside. For now it was enough just to be here, on the crest of the bluff, alone in the world with Royal. Neither the dark nor the woods frightened her. She knew the timber held nothing more dangerous than a possible skunk. It was slow going because of the dark, but they were in no hurry anyway.

Eventually Rhody's legs began to ache. She started to think about stopping to rest and eat, but she was afraid they were still too close to home.

Abruptly Royal halted. Barbed wire struck Rhody's knee. It was the downed boundary fence near her Indian mound.

"We'll stop there for a little while," she whispered as she held the fence down with her foot for Royal to jump over.

The clearing where the mound lay was just large enough to let in a shaft of moonlight. Rhody could see the black square of earth where the diggers had worked. She turned away from it and, in three long pulling steps, climbed the side of the mound. Royal leaped beside her.

"Here you go." She gave him two of the graham crackers. While he snatched them down, she twisted an Oreo cookie apart and scraped the white frosting off with her teeth. Her mother didn't let her eat them that way in front of people, but there was no Ora on the mound in the middle of the timber.

There was no one. No one except Rhoda Marie French and her dog.

Royal stretched out along Rhody's legs. He lay head up, watching her. He seemed curious.

"It's just you and me from now on," she said. She hadn't meant for her voice to sound even a little bit forlorn, but somehow it did.

After a long time she said, "This was probably a silly thing to do, wasn't it?"

He stretched out his head and laid it across her knees.

After another long time she said, quietly, "You're a dog. But I'm not."

A great heavy weariness pressed her down, down to the leaf-thick ground. She thought, I'll just rest for a few minutes, and then I'll decide . . .

Oddly, her last thought was not of running away, or of Royal. It was the feeling of momentary peace that had come in the veterinarian's office from leaning back into the solidness of her mother.

# Chapter 13

THE DOG dozed, too. After a time he woke and raised his head.

The girl was deep in sleep. He could hear it in the rhythm of her breathing and sense it in the softness of her muscles.

For a long time he lay looking at the girl, watching her eyes. Instincts were pulling at him, the same instincts that had made him try, time and again, to move on.

He felt a gentleness toward the girl. He felt, in some way that was new to him, attached to

her. But the older, deeper pulls made their inexorable demands on him.

He got up. For a long moment he stood over the girl, looking down at her, then looking off toward the river that lay to the east, the river where he went every year at this time, where rubber-booted men tossed him fish, and children fed him their sandwiches.

He lowered his head and touched the girl's neck, just the briefest touch, with his nose.

Then he was gone.

# If you liked this book you'll lik

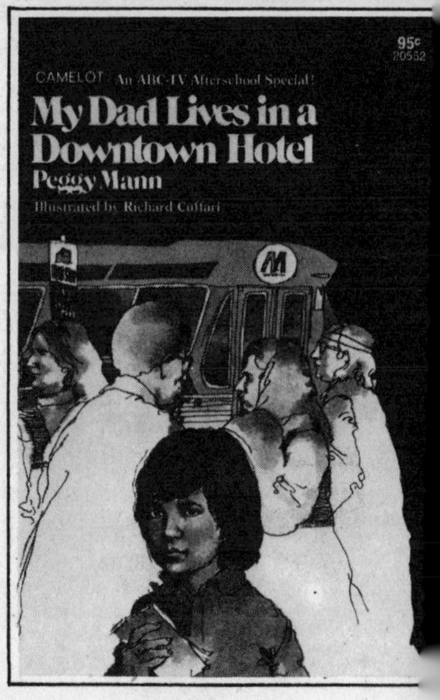


Camelot Books: distinguished paperbacks for people ages 7-14

**THE SUMMER OF THE SWANS**
Betsy Byars
A *Newbery Medal* winner.
Previously an *ABC Television Afterschool Special.* A fourteen-year-old girl deals with the resentment she feels over her mentally-retarded brother's dependency on her.
Illus. by Ted CoConis, **95¢**

**THE EIGHTEENTH EMERGENCY**
Betsy Byars
Betsy Byars portrays the child's sense of fantasy, fear and helplessness in this book about a little fellow who happens to provoke a big bully.
Previously an *ABC Television Afterschool Special.*
Illus. by Robert Grossman, **95¢**

**MY DAD LIVES IN A DOWNTOWN HOTEL**
Peggy Mann
A gentle and reassuring story for all children facing the trauma of a family break-up. MY DAD LIVES describes a ten-year-old boy's reactions to his parents' divorce. Previously an *ABC Television Afterschool Special.*
Illus. by Richard Cuffari, **95¢**

**THE WITCH WHO SAVED HALLOWEEN**
Marian T. Place
By the author of THE RESIDENT WITCH (Camelot Books' bestseller about Witcheena), this one is about Witchard — and the problems of pollution.
Illus. by Marilyn Miller, **95¢**

# hese other Camelot titles!

MYSTERY OF THE FOG MAN
Carol Farley
Winner of the Watts Mystery Award.
Illus., **95¢**

THE SNOWED-IN BOOK:
**More Stories from The Hollow Tree and Big Deep Woods**
Albert Bigelow Paine, Edited by Thom Roberts
More adventures — from the author of THE HOLLOW TREE — of the three forest friends, Coon, Possum, and Crow. Illus. by Cyndy Szekeres, **$1.25**

Also from Camelot:
THE MATTHEW LOONEY
series by Jerome Beatty, Jr., **95¢**
TUCKER'S COUNTRYSIDE
by George Selden, **95¢**
THE MOUSE AND HIS CHILD
by Russell Hoban, **95¢**
COCKLEBURR QUARTERS
by Charlotte Baker, **95¢**
**DORP DEAD** by Julia Cunningham, **95¢**
**KNEE-KNOCK RISE** by Natalie Babbitt, **95¢**

**CAMELOT**

Published by Avon Books
959 Eighth Avenue
New York, N.Y. 10019

A Camelot Books Catalog, a Camelot mobile, and a Camelot Study Guide are available on request.

# Camelot Books For Young Readers

## Specially for Boys

**THE INCREDIBLE DETECTIVES**
By Joan and Don Caulfield
*Illustrated by Kiyo Komoda.*
A trio of animal sleuths search the museum for their kidnapped boy, in a madcap frenzy of flying dinosaur bones and Egyptian mummies. **95¢**

**TIME CAT**
By Lloyd Alexander
Jason and his magical orange-eyed cat, Gareth, take off through the centuries for adventure in ancient lands. **95¢**

**THE HORSE THAT PLAYED CENTER FIELD**
By Hal Higdon
A bumbling ball team that's first with the fans and last in the league grabs the pennant, thanks to Oscar the Horse. **95¢**

## Specially for Girls

**THE WORLD IS ROUND**
By Gertrude Stein
*Illustrated by Clement Hurd.*
An enchanting "nonsense" book in which the famous writer immortalizes a little girl named Rose. **95¢**

**THE RESIDENT WITCH**
By Marian T. Place
*Illustrated by Marilyn Miller.*
Mischievous Witcheena is lonely and wants Earthlings to play with... and enters a public contest for Resident Witch to meet them! **95¢**

**MOKI**
By Grace Jackson Penney
*Illustrated by Gil Miret.*
Moki, a ten-year-old Cheyenne girl, saves a life—and finds her own kind of courage. **95¢**

A Camelot Books Catalog, a Camelot mobile, and a Camelot Study Guide are available on request.

Published by Avon Books
959 Eighth Avenue
New York, N.Y. 10019